It's Your First Day of School, Annie Claire

By Nancy White Carlstrom

Illustrated by Margie Moore

Abrams Books for Young Readers, New York

The illustrations in this book were made with black pen and watercolors on cold press paper.

Cataloging-in-Publication Data has been applied for
and may be obtained from the Library of Congress.
ISBN 978-0-8109-4057-4

Text copyright © 2009 Nancy White Carlstrom
Illustrations copyright © 2009 Margie Moore
Book design by Melissa Arnst

Printed and bound in China
10 9 8 7 6 5 4 3 2

Abrams Books for Young Readers are available at special discounts when purchased in quantity for premiums
and promotions as well as fundraising or educational use. Special editions can also be created to specification.
For details, contact specialmarkets@abramsbooks.com or the address below.

ABRAMS
THE ART OF BOOKS SINCE 1949
115 West 18th Street
New York, NY 10011
www.abramsbooks.com

For the Mikuta family: Sandra, Larry, Trinity, Marjorie, and Ruth
—Nancy White Carlstrom

For my sister, Mary
—Margie Moore

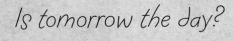
Is tomorrow the day?

Yes it is, my dear.
The first day of school
Will finally be here.

But what if I'm too tired
And stay in my bed?

I'll say, "Get up now,
Annie Claire, Sleepyhead!"

What if I spill my milk
All over the floor?

We'll just clean it up—
It's happened before.

Love you, my messy Annie Claire.

But what if I want you
To sit in my chair
And be at my school
With your Annie Claire?

You know, Annie Claire,
Your mama's too tall
And won't really fit
In a chair that's so small.

You'll sit down and see
It's just right for you,
And I'll stay for a while
If you want me to.

What if others can sing
And color and count
And I can't do anything
But shout, shout, shout?

Annie Claire, when you're loud,
Your teacher might say,
"Use an inside voice—
It's much better that way."

Love you, my noisy Annie Claire.

What if at story time
I sleep and I snore

And everyone laughs
And I just snore some more?

And I slip and I slide
And fall off of my chair,
My hands on the floor
And my feet in the air!

Teacher will say,
"Annie Claire, Sleepyhead,
Remember tonight
It's early to bed."

Love you, my sleepy Annie Claire.

What if no one will play
Or be friends with me
And I'm all alone
Sitting under that tree?

Some of your old friends
Already wait
There in your classroom—
Let's not be late.

Mama, what if you're sad
And can't eat your lunch
'Cause you're home all alone
And miss me a bunch?

Come here, let me kiss you—
Kisses one, two, and three.
I know I will miss you
And you will miss me.

We will get used to this.
We both have to try.
It will be OK.

But why, Mama, why?

Because, Annie Claire,
I will always love you.
No matter what happens
Or what you might do.

My love stays with you
Wherever you are—
Whenever I'm near you,
Whenever I'm far.

It's your first day of school,
Annie Claire. Don't you know
My love's always with you
Wherever you go.

Love you, my one and only Annie Claire.